For Rich and my
Moon, TBFIL x - B. D.

For Evie May - D. B.

tiger tales
5 River Road, Suite 128, Wilton, CT 06897
Published in the United States 2021
Originally published in Great Britain 2021
by Little Tiger Press Ltd.
Text by Becky Davies · Illustrations by Dana Brown
Text and illustrations copyright © 2021 Little Tiger Press Ltd.
ISBN-13: 978-1-68010-263-5
ISBN-10: 1-68010-263-X
Printed in China · LTP/2800/3733/0521
All rights reserved · 10 9 8 7 6 5 4 3 2 1

www.tigertalesbooks.com

The Forest Stewardship Council® (FSC®) is an international,
non-governmental organization dedicated to promoting responsible
management of the world's forests. FSC® operates a system of forest
certification and product labeling that allows consumers to identify
wood and wood-based products from well-managed forests.

For more information about the FSC®, please visit their website at www.fsc.org

FSC
www.fsc.org
MIX
Paper from
responsible sources
FSC® C017606

I Love You More than All the Stars

by Becky Davies

Illustrated by Dana Brown

tiger tales

I love you more than all the **STARS** that shimmer in the night.

Just as their glow lights up the sky, my love shines **STRONG** and **BRIGHT.**

...ove you more than

SUMMER

DAYS

...I more than

SUNSETS, TOO.

I love you deeper than the sea, its waves of ENDLESS BLUE.

I love you STRONGER

And

softer

than a

snowflake

dance

as crystals gently twirl.

I love you

HIGHER

than the

CLOUDS...

...and sweeter than the

B I Z R A R

I love you further
than the
MOON
and then back
home again.

I love you
LONGER
than a
day . . .

. . . a week, a month, a year.
My love lasts for eternity.

Forever I'll be here.

I love you wider than the WORLD that shimmers down below.

You're my best friend.

I LOVE YOU

more than you

will ever know.